Goodnight Baby Bear

Michael Shoulders

Illustrated by Teri Weidner

Sleeping Bear Press™

2395 South Huron Parkway, Suite 200
Ann Arbor, MI 48104
www.sleepingbearpress.com

Printed and bound in the United States.

10 9 8 7 6 5 4

Library of Congress Cataloging-in-Publication Data

Shoulders, Michael.
Goodnight Baby Bear / written by Michael Shoulders;
illustrated by Teri Weidner.
p. cm.
Summary: Nightly, the members of a bear family that value books and reading
share a personally inscribed book and a cookie with Baby Bear to celebrate milestones
and memorable days in his life. Includes recipe for honey oatmeal raisin cookies.
ISBN 978-1-58536-471-8
[1. Bears—Fiction. 2. Books and reading—Fiction. 3. Family life—Fiction.] I. Weidner,
Teri, ill. II. Title.
PZ7.S558833Go 2010
[E]—dc22
2009036938

For Beverly Bullock and Judy Morgan who know one of the most
precious gifts we can give to those we love is a book!
and
For Michelle and Kyllean Browne who inspired this story.
"I thank you to the moon and back!"

MIKE

For Lily and Olivia Weidner

TERI

Momma Bear loves Baby Bear more than
she loves honey oatmeal raisin cookies.
And she really loves honey oatmeal raisin cookies.

Baby Bear has fun watching butterflies with Momma.

He and Momma Bear plant butterfly bushes in the field at the edge of the next woods.

They picnic while swallowtails and skippers dance on splashes of purple, red, and white.

They build houses to keep their friends warm at night.

When Momma tucks him into bed, Baby Bear gets one honey oatmeal raisin cookie and picks one special book.

June 9

For Baby Bear,
To remember making friends
with the butterflies.
May you grow to love
as much as you are loved.
Momma

By the time Momma reads, "Nobody ever called him an ugly caterpillar again!" Baby Bear is fast asleep.

Good night, Baby Bear.

Daddy Bear loves Baby Bear more than he loves honey oatmeal raisin cookies. And he really loves honey oatmeal raisin cookies. Baby Bear has fun on the farm with Daddy.

Daddy needs help hooking the tractor to the trailer.

Daddy can't dig a hole for the acorn without help.

And Daddy can't find his way back to the barn so Baby Bear steers the blue tractor all by himself.

When Daddy tucks him into bed, Baby Bear gets one honey oatmeal raisin cookie and picks one special book.

MARCH 28

FOR BABY BEAR,

TO REMEMBER THE DAY

WE PLANTED A MIGHTY OAK.

LOVE,
DADDY

By the time Daddy reads, "As time passed, birds, squirrels, and honeybees called the tree home, thanks to a tiny acorn!" Baby Bear is fast asleep.

Good night, Baby Bear.

Brother Bear loves his brother more than he loves honey oatmeal raisin cookies. And he really loves honey oatmeal raisin cookies. Baby Bear has fun at the beach with his brother.

Brother Bear chases him
with crabs.

Brother Bear remembers
to bring bubbles.

And Brother Bear helps him sail a
kite in the soft ocean breeze.

When Brother tucks him into bed, Baby Bear gets one honey oatmeal raisin cookie and picks one special book.

Together like oceans and waves,
Together like kites and wind,
Together like sand and beaches,
I'll always be your bestest friend

August 22

Bubba

By the time Brother reads, "The dolphins never worried about evil sea serpents again!" Baby Bear is fast asleep.

Good night, Baby Bear.

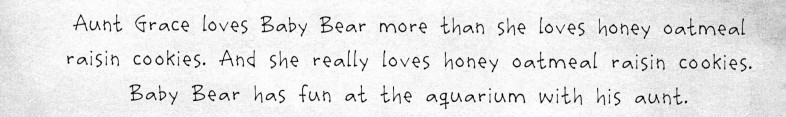

Aunt Grace loves Baby Bear more than she loves honey oatmeal raisin cookies. And she really loves honey oatmeal raisin cookies. Baby Bear has fun at the aquarium with his aunt.

He asks lots of questions:
"How come stingrays have
pointy tails?"

"How come sharks
never sleep?"

And, Aunt Grace takes funny
pictures of Baby Bear.

When Aunt Grace tucks him into bed, Baby Bear gets one honey oatmeal raisin cookie and picks one special book.

December 28

For Baby Bear,
to remember our first trip
to the aquarium.
Learn, grow, and know!
Hugs, Aunt Grace

By the time Aunt Grace reads, "Mr. Octopus won
the hugging contest!" Baby Bear is fast asleep.

Good night, Baby Bear.

Uncle Roy loves Baby Bear more than he loves honey oatmeal raisin cookies. And he really loves honey oatmeal raisin cookies. Baby Bear has fun dressing in Uncle Roy's clown suit.

Uncle Roy paints a
smile on his face.

Uncle Roy puts a big red
ball on the tip of his nose.

And Uncle Roy shows him how
to make a scarf disappear.

When Uncle Roy tucks him into bed, Baby Bear gets one honey oatmeal raisin cookie and picks one special book.

To my nephew
"Pockets-The-clown!"   April 24

Knock-Knock!
Who's there?
POLICE!
Police who?

Police don't eat honey oatmeal
raisin cookies without me!
Ha-ha,
Uncle Roy

By the time Uncle Roy reads, "The king laughed so hard
his pajamas fell off!" Baby Bear is fast asleep.

Good night, Baby Bear.

Nana loves Baby Bear more than
she loves honey oatmeal raisin cookies.

Best of all, she loves eating honey oatmeal
raisin cookies with Baby Bear!

She tucks him into bed and catches up
on all she's missed since her last visit....

Nana reads, *Bucky Beaver Gets a Tooth.*
"I got that book when I got these,"
he says. "My, what big teeth you
have!" Nana says.

Nana reads, *Tadpole Gets Sick.*
"I got that book when I got a
shot right here," Baby Bear says.

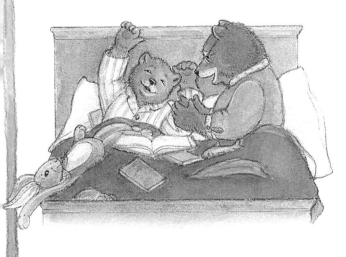

Nana reads, *Baby Bird Tries His
Wings.* "I got that book when
I took my first step!"

Nana reads one special book she brought with her.

Just after she reads, "And they all loved
happily ever after!" they both fall fast asleep.

Good night, Baby Bear.

Beary Special Honey Oatmeal Raisin Cookies

2 cups rolled oats, blend 1 cup in blender

1/2 cup honey

3/4 cup brown sugar

1 cup shortening or butter

1 tsp. salt

1 cup flour

2 eggs

4 tbsp. milk with 1 tsp. baking soda added to it

1 cup raisins (or nuts, optional)

Cream together sugar and butter or shortening. Add eggs, honey, salt, milk, and soda. Mix. Add flour, mix again. Stir in oats and raisins or nuts. Refrigerate dough 1 hour. Drop by spoonfuls onto greased cookie sheet. Bake at 350 degrees Fahrenheit for 10-12 minutes.

Enjoy!